YOU CAN'T BE TOO CAREFUL!

ROGER MELLO

Translated by Daniel Hahn

Para Marcelo, que chegou antes, a tempo de embaralhar as horas

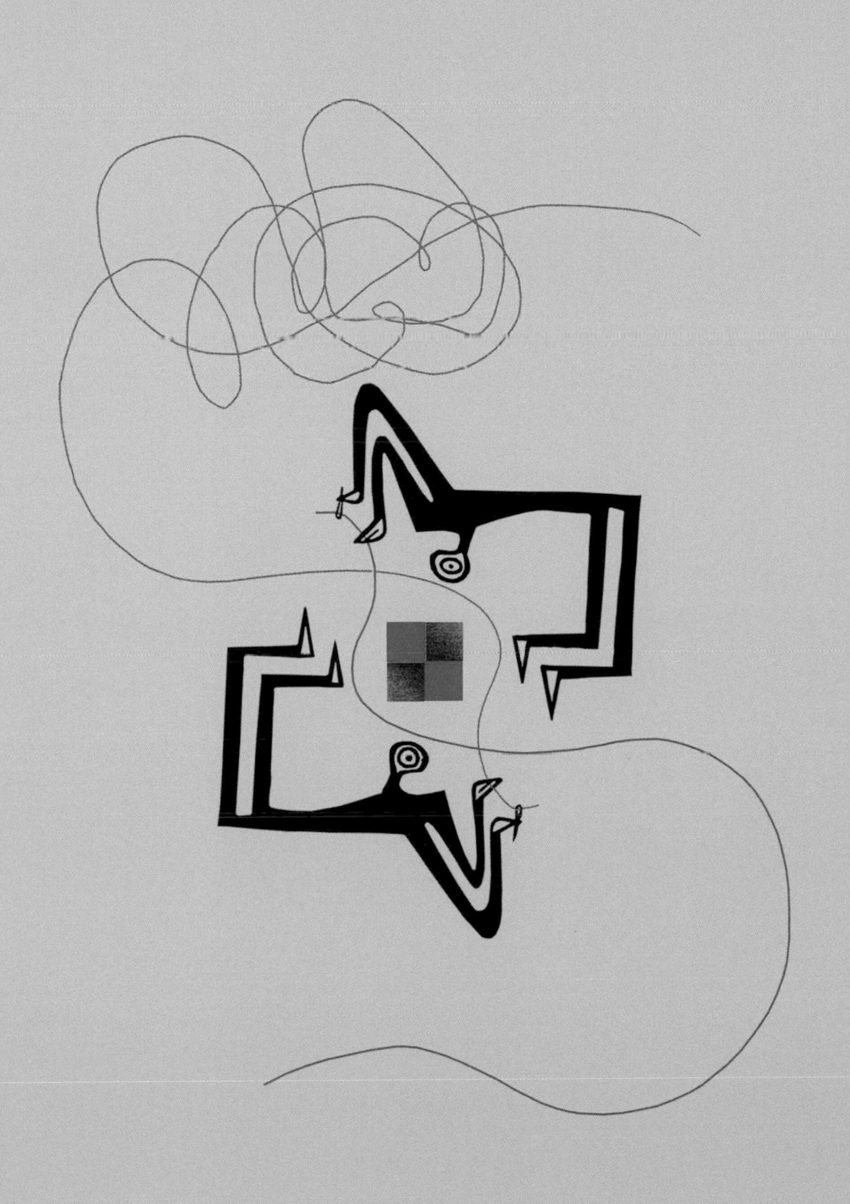

White Rose is safely in her pen.
The gardener is keeping a close eye on her.
The gardener doesn't turn away for a single moment
as if White Rose might escape from her pen.

BUT YOU CAN'T BE TOO CAREFUL...

The gardener will not leave his post. He won't go outside, not even if it pours with rain and the washing gets soaked on the line, as he woke this morning with a rather nasty cold.

He caught a cold from having spent so long barefoot trying to find his shoes.

Which the cat had hidden.

He'd been given this cat by the youngest of his brothers.

The youngest of his brothers was married to Dalva, who had inherited the cat from an uncle.

The love letter had been sent, but it fell out of the mailman's sack...

At the very moment when the mailman bent down to pick up a brass ring.

The brass ring had ended up on the sidewalk when the seamstress threw it out of her window, telling her fiancé that she would not marry him "for all the gold in the world!"

Unless he got rid of that ridiculous moustache.

Dalva's uncle had died of sorrow waiting for a love letter that never came.

He had grown the ridiculous moustache because of a promise made by his mother, an opera singer. Who had almost lost her voice from shouting Help! Help! Help! when she fell down the hole.

The hole had been dug to bury the old man who had been hovering between life and death. But he did not die. (He only didn't die because of the performing monkey who went to live with him and brought him his medicine.)

The performing monkey used to work in the circus, then ran away.

"Why did he run away?" asked the circus owner.

"The clown stepped on his tail when he ran past."

"I ran because I heard a noise," said the clown.

The noise of the world falling on the floor.

AND THE WORLD WAS KEPT RIGHT ON TOP OF THE MANAGER'S DESK.
IT WAS A GIFT FROM HIS ANNOYING COUSIN.

"From now on, the value of gold will depend on its weight, not on the craftsmanship," decreed the man who owned the scales.

The goldsmith no longer made brooches with the great care he used to. Because no one took any interest in his work any more.

His cousin was annoying because she wore a gold brooch that kept pricking her.

That was how he wanted it, because the scales were his. And that's that.

The owner had bought the scales from Agripino, the wealthiest man in the world, who had chosen to give himself up to adventure and had lost everything.

Agripino had lost everything along the way when he journeyed to Mauritania on the back of a shining bird. And kidnapped the Emir's daughter...

...Who had very much wanted to be kidnapped, so much so that she had sent out the shining bird to bring back the first adventurer it could find.

The shining bird had been presented to her as a wedding gift by Rajah The Malodorous.

The Rajah had become malodorous from spending so much time bathing in herbs and sour milk. A prescription from a fake doctor to help him marry more quickly.

The fake doctor was called Onofre, and he had never graduated. One year earlier, he'd jumped the wall of the medical school.

He jumped the wall because he didn't want to be a doctor. He dreamed of playing the bagpipes.

But his father would not allow it. "Everyone who learns to play the bagpipes ends up wearing a skirt!" he said.

His father was very old-fashioned.

Perhaps because he never read the papers.

Which the newsagent didn't deliver, because he didn't know the way.

The way was on a map. But nobody could get their bearings because the compass rose had disappeared.

The compass rose had vanished off the map.

"Who's hidden the compass?"
And somebody replied in a whisper:
"It was White Rose. It was White Rose."

But hang on a moment...

White Rose is safely in her pen.
So White Rose did not hide the compass.

And the compass is still on the map.

The map led the newsagent to the house of Onofre's father.

Who always keeps up-to-date with his newspapers and is a very open-minded sort of fellow. He even bought his son some bagpipes.

Onofre plays those bagpipes like you wouldn't believe! He was invited to perform for the Rajah.

The Rajah got so excited about the music that he decided to take several baths with sandalwood and aromatic herbs.

From here to distant lands there is no bachelor more eligible than Rajah The Intoxicating. But his first wife was to be the daughter of the Emir of Mauritania.

The Emir's daughter eagerly awaited her wedding, marking the days on her calendar with sapphires. Her future husband gave her a shining bird, which she locked in a cage so it would never escape.

The bird never flew to Agripino, who's still the wealthiest man in the world, though he does occasionally think about giving himself up to adventure.

Nobody bought Agripino's scales, which anyway were never for sale, as he's really very attached to his things. And that's that.

"WHAT'S THE POINT OF ALL THESE CARATS OF GOLD WITHOUT A BEAUTIFUL DESIGN?" THOUGHT THE GOLDSMITH, AS HE FINISHED WORK ON ONE MORE BROOCH, WHICH HE CRAFTED WITH THE GREATEST OF CARE.

THIS DELICATE BROOCH DOES NOT HURT THE CIRCUS MANAGER'S COUSIN. SHE IS AN EXTREMELY PLEASANT WOMAN, WHO TRAVELS THE WHOLE WORLD COLLECTING POSTCARDS.

SHE HAS NEVER EVEN MET HER COUSIN THE MANAGER.

Her cousin the manager has been busy dealing with all the paperwork for the candidacy of an ex-clown.

Who has "had it up to here" with the circus.

"What a dull life," said the clown. "I'm going into politics!"

And off he went.

(He'd been jealous of the performing monkey, who remains the main attraction to this day.)

The performing monkey never met the old man, who ended up dying.

And was buried.

The opera singer went to the funeral. Her song of farewell drew such sighs from all the people there.

She has the voice of an angel!

And she has a son with no moustache.

Who is married to the seamstress, who likes to show off her brass ring to everyone she meets.

Even to the mailman.

"What a lovely ring!" he said.

Then he dashed off to deliver a love letter.

THE LOVE LETTER REACHED THE MAN, WHOSE LIFE TODAY IS A GLORIOUS DREAM.

MEANWHILE HIS CAT SLEEPS.

THE MAN IS DALVA'S UNCLE.

SHE WAS MARRIED TO THE YOUNGEST OF THE GARDENER'S BROTHERS.

The gardener always, always wears his shoes. And he has never caught a cold.

From right up close, the gardener watches White Rose.

He doesn't turn away for a single moment.

As if White Rose might escape from her pen.

But then it began to rain...

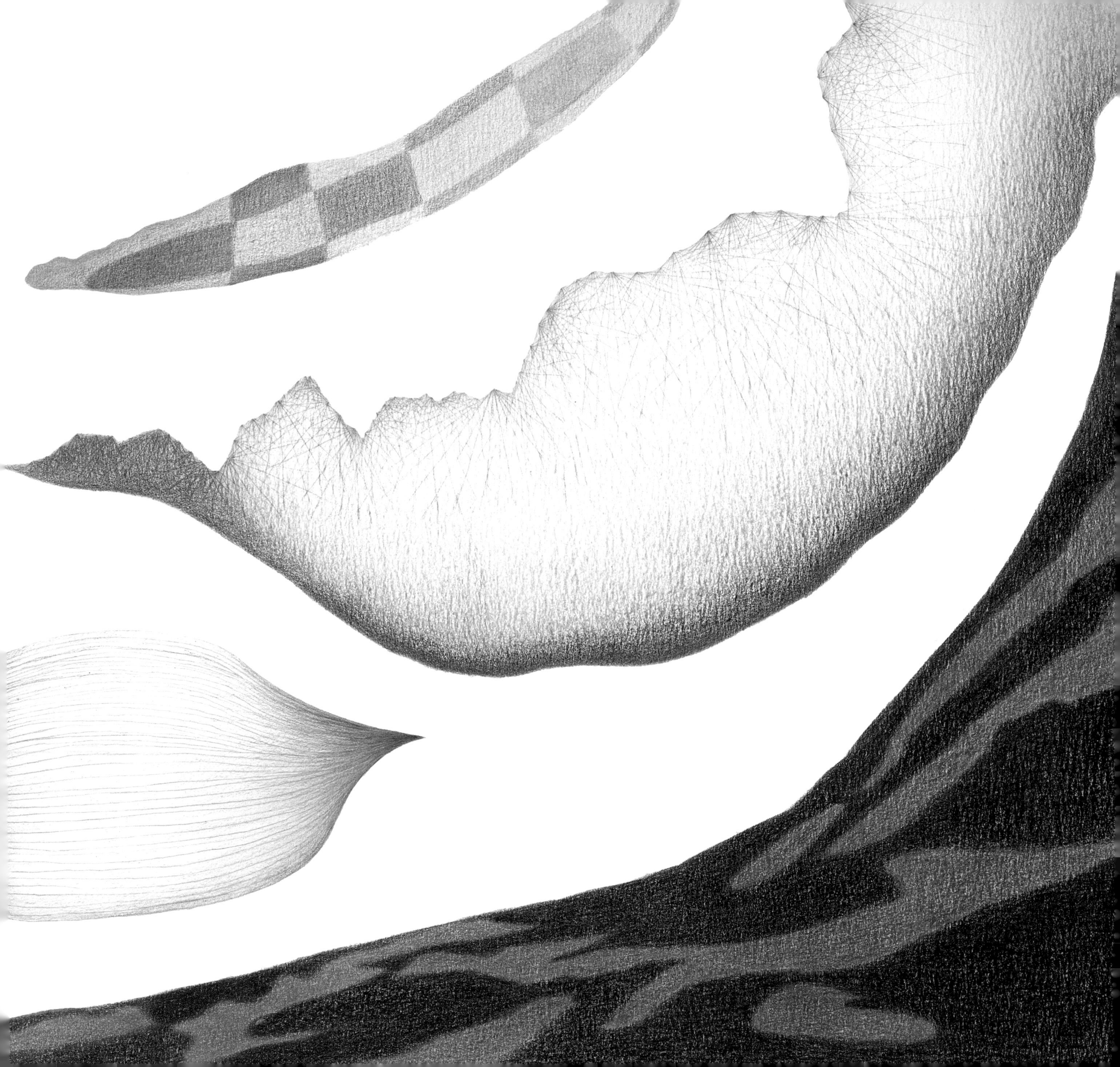

THE GARDENER RUSHED OUT INTO THE RAIN TO FETCH THE WASHING FROM THE LINE.

When he came back, he couldn't believe his eyes.
White Rose had escaped from her pen.

Originally published as *Todo cuidado é pouco!* by Companhia das Letras, Sao Paolo

First Elsewhere Editions Printing, 2017

Library of Congress Cataloging-in-Publication Data
Mello, Roger, author, illustrator. | Hahn, Daniel, translator.
You can't be too careful! / Roger Mello ; translated by Daniel Hahn.
Todo cuidado é pouco! English | You cannot be too careful!
LCCN 2016025198 (print) | LCCN 2016041802 (ebook)
ISBN 978-0-914671-64-0 (hardback) | ISBN 978-0-914671-65-7 (E-book)

Elsewhere Editions
232 3rd Street #A111
Brooklyn, NY 11215

Distributed by Penguin Random House
www.penguinrandomhouse.com

This publication was made possible with support from
the Ministério da Cultura do Brasil / Fundação Biblioteca Nacional,
Lannan Foundation, the Amazon Literary Partnership,
the Nimick Forbesway Foundation, the National Endowment for the Arts,
the New York State Council on the Arts, a state agency,
and the New York City Department of Cultural Affairs.

MINISTÉRIO DA CULTURA
Fundação BIBLIOTECA NACIONAL

PRINTED IN CANADA

Winner of the 2014 Hans Christian Andersen Award, **ROGER MELLO** has illustrated over 100 titles – 22 of which he also wrote – and his unique style and adroit sense of color continues to push the boundaries of children's book illustration. Mello has dedicated his life to exploring the history and culture of Brazil through children's illustrated stories. Rather than relying on written narrative to tell the story, he invites his young readers to fill the gaps with imagination. Mello has won numerous awards for writing and illustrating, including three of IBBY's Luís Jardim Awards, nine Concours Best Illustration Awards, and the Best Children's Book 2002 International Award.

DANIEL HAHN is the author of a number of works of nonfiction, including The Tower Menagerie. He is one of the editors of The Ultimate Book Guide, a series of reading guides for children and teenagers. His translation of The Book of Chameleons by José Eduardo Agualusa won the Independent Foreign Fiction Prize in 2007 and his translation of Agualusa's A General Theory of Oblivion was shortlisted for the Man Booker International Prize in 2016. He has translated the work of Philippe Claudel, María Duenas, José Saramago, Eduardo Halfon, and others. In 2015 he published the new Oxford Companion to Children's Literature.

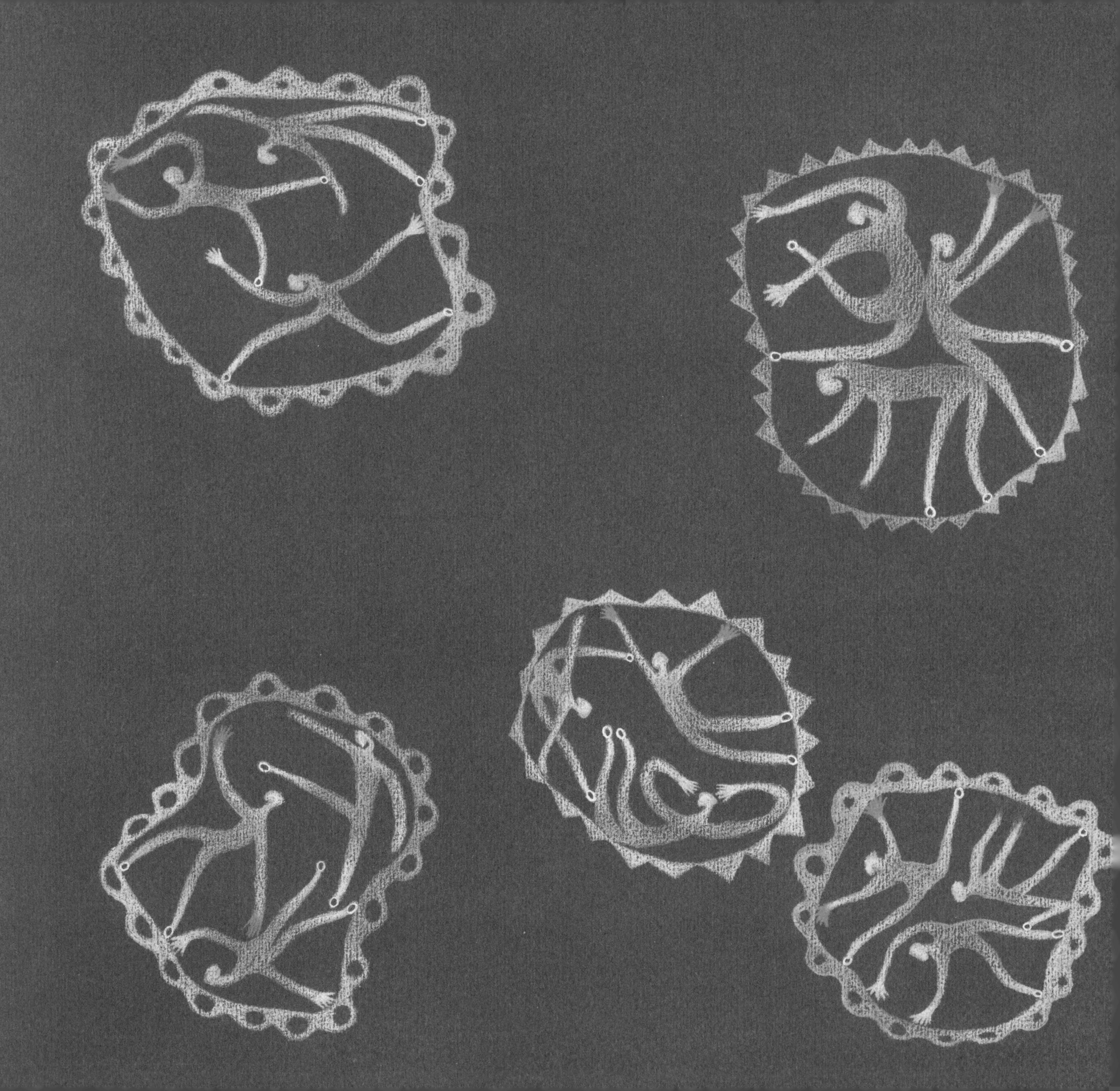